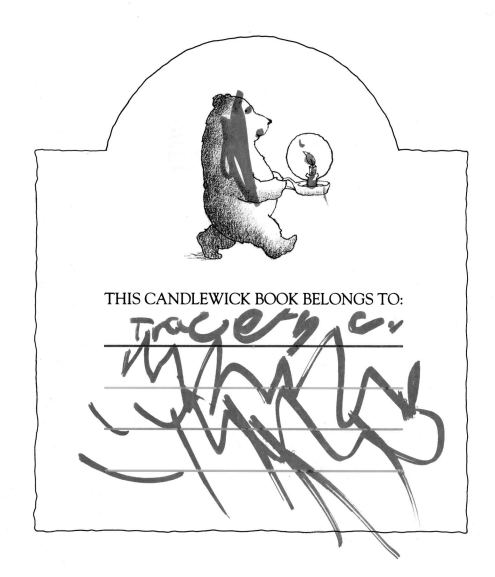

THIS CANDLEWICK BOOK BELONGS TO:

Tracey C.

Baby Animals

Five Stories of Endangered Species

For Spencer and Serena
D. H.

For Joanna and Lucy
J. B.

Baby Animals

Five Stories of Endangered Species

by Derek Hall

illustrated by John Butler

CANDLEWICK PRESS

CAMBRIDGE, MASSACHUSETTS

First U.S. paperback edition in this form 1994.

First published individually in Great Britain as
Panda Climbs (1984), *Tiger Runs* (1984), *Elephant Bathes* (1985),
Polar Bear Leaps (1985), *Gorilla Builds* (1985) by
Walker Books Ltd., 87 Vauxhall Walk, London SE11 5HJ.

Library of Congress Cataloging-in-Publication Data
Hall, Derek, 1930-
Baby animals: five stories of endangered species / Derek Hall; illustrated by John Butler.
Summary: Presents five brief stories about babies of endangered species, illustrating how they play, what
they eat, how they interact with their mothers and fathers, and how they learn to survive in the wild.
ISBN 1-56402-004-5 (hardcover)—ISBN 1-56402-362-1 (paperback)
1. Animals—Infancy—Juvenile fiction. 2. Children's stories. English. [1. Animals—Infancy—Fiction.
2. Rare animals—Fiction. 3. Short stories.] I. Butler, John, 1952- ill II. Title.
PZ10.3.H142Bab 1992
[E]—dc20
91-71861

2 4 6 8 10 9 7 5 3 1

Printed in Hong Kong

The pictures in this book were done in acrylic paint.

Candlewick Press
2067 Massachusetts Avenue
Cambridge, Massachusetts 02140

Contents

Balega
the Elephant

Balega is playing while his mother munches leaves. He runs around shaking his head and waggling his ears.

What's that? Balega sees something moving in an old tree. He carefully stretches out his trunk and puts the tip inside a hole.

Ouch! Balega jumps back. Something has
stung him and it hurts. Suddenly hornets
come flying out, buzzing
around him angrily.

Balega runs back to his mother, squealing.
He is frightened. She gently strokes his
face with her trunk to make him
feel better.

Balega and his mother go down to the pool.
They both drink, sucking up water in their
trunks and squirting it down their throats.

Balega's mother rolls over on her side.
Balega tries to climb on top of her but keeps
slipping and sliding off. It's really fun.

They have a wonderful time splashing and swishing
around with their trunks. Then Balega squirts
water over his mother. She likes it, too!

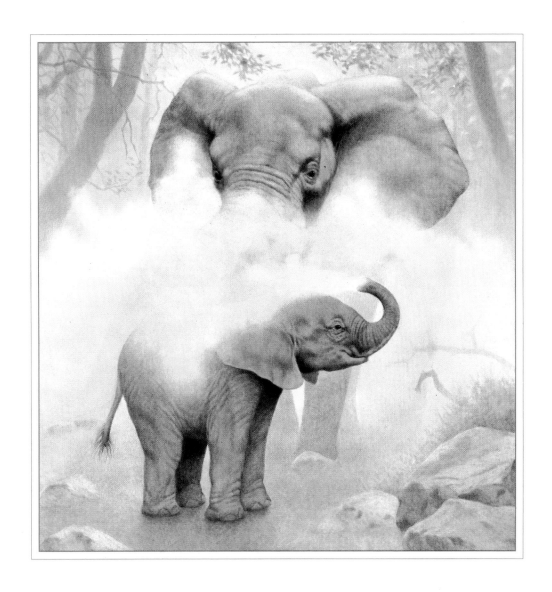

After their bath, they blow dust over themselves.
It sticks to their wet skins and keeps them cool.
Best of all, it stops insects from biting!

Khana
the Tiger

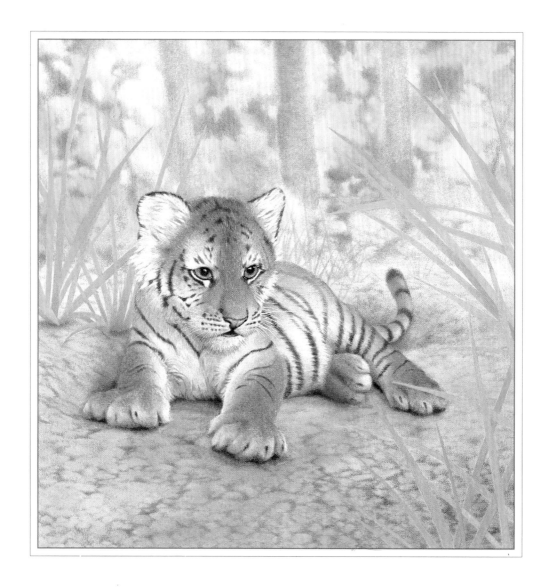

Khana is feeling so bored. Her mother has gone
hunting for food. Hunting is very dangerous, so
Khana must stay in a safe place.

Khana wants to play. What's that? Something is
moving in the grass. She trots over to see.
It's a beautiful butterfly.

Khana tries to touch the butterfly, but it darts
away. She scampers after it.
Again and again she tries
to catch it with her paw.

Khana is lost! She has chased the
butterfly for such a long way.
And now it is raining. She sits
down and cries like a kitten.

Suddenly there's a noise! Khana looks up, frightened. A huge elephant is lumbering toward her. It's the biggest animal she has ever seen.

Khana turns and runs faster than she has
ever run before. She is running like
the wind, and crying for
her mother.

Khana hears her mother's roar and runs to meet her. Khana's mother is very angry. But Khana is so pleased to see her again.

Khana's mother soon forgives her. They lie
down, and Khana climbs onto her. She purrs
happily, feeling safe once more.

Chi-li
the Panda

Chi-li loves to play with his mother. Sometimes
she gives him a piggyback ride and then he
feels as tall as a grown-up panda.

Soon it is dinnertime. The grown-ups eat lots of
bamboo shoots, crunching the juicy stems.
Chi-li likes to chew the soft leaves.

The grown-ups eat for such a long time and always fall asleep afterward. Chi-li scampers off to play. He rolls over and over in the snow and tumbles down a hill.

When Chi-li stops at the bottom,
he cannot see his mother anymore.
But he sees a leopard! Chi-li is
very frightened.

He scrambles over to the nearest tree and
climbs up. Chi-li has never climbed before,
and it is so easy! He digs his claws into
the bark and goes up and up.

Soon he is near the top. Chi-li feels so good
up here. And he can see such a long way over
the mountains and trees and snow of China.

Chi-li hears his mother crying. She is looking for him. He starts to climb down. But going down is harder than climbing up, and he slips. Plop! He lands in the snow.

Chi-li's mother is so happy. She gathers him up in her big furry arms and cuddles him. It is wonderful to be warm and safe with her again.

Laska
the Polar Bear

Laska the polar bear is big enough to leave
the den where he was born. For the first time
he plays outside in the soft snow.

Soon it is time to go to the sea for food. Laska's mother is hungry. He rides high on her back, gripping her fur with excitement.

While his mother is busy eating, Laska wanders off. He stands up on his hind legs, as tall as he can, to look out over the Arctic Ocean.

Suddenly the ice breaks! A small ice floe carries Laska away from the land, and he is too young to swim! He whimpers for his mother.

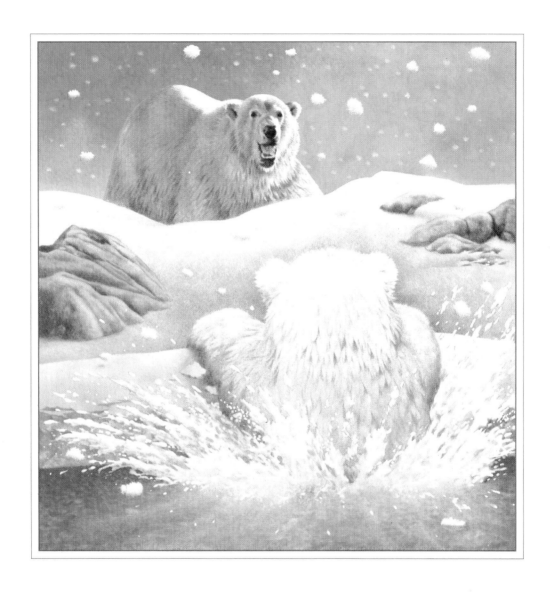

She roars to her cub in alarm. Bravely he
leaps across the gap toward her.
It is almost too far! His paws
slither on the icy shore.

Just in time his mother grasps him by the neck. She hauls him, dripping wet, from the water. Laska hangs limp and miserable from her strong jaws.

On firm land again, he shakes himself like
a dog to dry his fur. His mother wants
to find a safe place to sleep. Laska
follows her like a shadow.

Now Laska is hungry. His mother feeds him
with her milk. Then he snuggles up to her
warm body and goes to sleep.

Simbi
the Gorilla

Simbi and her father finish their dinner in the forest. She has eaten lots of tasty leaves. He likes to chew on juicy stalks as well.

Simbi's father is sleepy and decides to make a
nest. He bends stalks and leaves and walks on
them until they are soft. Simbi watches.

Her father settles back on the nest, wriggling around and stretching until he is comfortable. Poor Simbi—there's no room for her!

Simbi decides to make her own nest. She climbs
a tree near her father and rocks backward and
forward on it. It's fun—it's like a swing.

But Simbi is a little too heavy. And the tree is a little too thin. It suddenly bends right over and Simbi slips. She is falling. . . .

She lands on top of her father and wakes
him up. He scrambles to his feet, grumpy
and grumbling. Simbi hurries away.

Simbi climbs a stronger tree. She bends leafy twigs and branches. Then she tramples on them to make a soft cushion of leaves.

Simbi has done it—made her first nest high up
in a tree! She snuggles down and nibbles some
more leaves. Simbi feels just like a grown-up.

Natural history notes

Elephants like Balega live in Africa. Mother elephants and their families travel around in groups called herds. Most of the grown-up members of the herd are sisters. Elephants have only one baby at a time, so Balega probably plays with cousins his own age, not with his older brothers and sisters. A little elephant will stay with his mother's herd for twelve years or more; by then he will be nearly grown up.

Tigers like Khana live in India and nearby hot countries, though a few are found in cold northern forests. A mother tiger usually has a family of three or four cubs–sometimes as many as six. She feeds them on milk for several months, then helps them learn how to hunt other animals. Khana and her brothers and sisters will stay with their mother until they are nearly three years old. By this time they will be good hunters, and able to fend for themselves.

Giant pandas like Chi-li live on the slopes of high mountains in China. They are among the rarest animals in the world, and because of this they have become the symbol for the World Wide Fund for Nature. Mother pandas usually have one baby at a time and care for it for about six months. Then the young panda leaves to search for food on its own. The panda has a special extra thumb on each of its front feet, which helps it to hold the bamboo shoots that it eats.

Polar bears like Laska live near the sea in the far north of the world. At the beginning of the winter, the mother polar bear digs a deep den in the snow. Her three or four babies, who are the size of guinea pigs, are born there at about Christmastime. They stay warmly cuddled up to her and feed on her milk for about three months–then they are big enough to venture out of the den. Polar bears stay with their mothers for two to three years. By then they are large and can hunt for themselves.

Simbi and her father, like all other wild gorillas, live in Africa. Though they are large, gorillas are peaceable animals. Family groups travel around a home area in forests near the equator, looking for the plants they like to eat. They also spend a good deal of time resting. All gorillas can climb quite well, but the big males, like Simbi's father, usually make comfortable beds on the ground. Baby gorillas generally sleep beside their mothers until they are about two years old, but they do practice making nests for themselves. Simbi's playmates are probably her cousins, for her mother is not likely to have another baby until Simbi is about four years old.

DEREK HALL has worked as a surveyor, interviewer, journalist, actor, and editor, and has trained as an architect. He has written short stories and plays for radio and television, as well as nonfiction for children.

JOHN BUTLER has designed and illustrated sixteen books on wildlife and contributed to many more. His work has been exhibited and published in both the United States and Europe, and his commissions include work for the Natural History Museum in London and the World Wide Fund for Nature.